How Oliver Olson
Changed the World

Also by Claudia Mills

SQUARE
FISH

An Imprint of Macmillan

Library of Congress Cataloging-in-Publication Data
Mills, Claudia.
    How Oliver Olson changed the world / Claudia Mills ; pictures by
Heather Maione.
        p.   cm.
    Summary: Afraid he will always be an outsider like ex-planet
Pluto, nine-year-old Oliver finally shows his extremely overprotective
parents that he is capable of doing great things without their help
while his class is studying the solar system.
    ISBN 978-0-312-67282-9
    [1. Parenting—Fiction.   2. Self-realization—Fiction.   3. Solar
system—Fiction.   4. Science projects—Fiction.   5. Diorama—
Fiction.   6. Schools—Fiction.   7. Legislators—Fiction.
8. Colorado—Fiction.]   I. Maione, Heather Harms, ill.   II. Title.

PZ7.M63963 How 2009
[Fic]—dc22

                                                        2007048846

Originally published in the United States by Farrar Straus Giroux
First Square Fish Edition: October 2011
Square Fish logo designed by Filomena Tuosto
Book designed by Jonathan Bartlett
mackids.com

10   9   8   7   6   5   4   3   2   1

AR: 4.7 / LEXILE: 730L

How Oliver Olson
Changed the World

Claudia Mills
Pictures by Heather Maione

SQUARE
FISH

Farrar Straus Giroux
New York

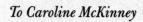

To Caroline McKinney

How Oliver Olson
Changed the World

1

Oliver Olson looked up at the moon.

The large inflated ball hung on a string from the ceiling in Mrs. O'Neill's third-grade classroom. Earth and Mars and the other planets hung there, too, because this was the Monday that Oliver's class was starting its five-week study of outer space.

"When I was a girl," Mrs. O'Neill said, "astronauts walked on the moon for the very first time."

Oliver tried to imagine Mrs. O'Neill as a girl. The best he could do was picture a much shorter version of a stout, short-haired lady with thick glasses and a kind smile.

"How many of you would like to walk on the moon?"

Every hand shot up, except for Oliver's. Oliver's parents would never let him walk on the moon. The moon was too far away. It was too cold. It didn't have enough gravity. The rocket might explode. Rockets exploded all the time.

Mrs. O'Neill looked at Oliver. He hoped she wouldn't ask him why he didn't want to walk on the moon. She didn't.

But Crystal Harding did. Her desk was right next to Oliver's. "Why don't you want to walk on the moon?" she whispered.

Oliver shrugged.

A shrug wasn't enough of an answer for Crystal. "Do you think it's dangerous?"

Oliver nodded. Maybe a nod would end the conversation.

"Flying is safer than driving a car," Crystal said. "It's even safer than riding a bike."

Well, being launched into outer space in a rocket wasn't the same thing as flying. And Oliver's parents were never going to let him drive a car, either. They didn't even let him ride a bike with his friend J. P. Gleason, except for around and around their boring little cul-de-sac.

"Crystal?" Mrs. O'Neill said.

"I was just asking Oliver why he didn't want to walk on the moon." Now everyone was staring at Oliver. "And he said it was dangerous." Actually, Oliver hadn't *said* anything. "And then I said—"

"Crystal." Mrs. O'Neill interrupted her gently but firmly. "Right now I need you to be listening, not talking."

Crystal gave Mrs. O'Neill an apologetic smile. At least five times a day, Mrs. O'Neill had to remind Crystal about not talking. She was the most talkative person Oliver had ever known.

"Astronauts first walked on the moon on July 20, 1969," Mrs. O'Neill told the class. "Neil Armstrong led the way, and he spoke the first words ever spoken on the moon. He said, 'That's one small step for a man, one giant leap for mankind.' "

Oliver thought Neil Armstrong must have planned what to say ahead of time. Those words didn't sound like something that would pop into someone's head on the spur of the moment. Maybe Neil Armstrong's parents had written them for him and made him memorize them.

J.P. raised his hand. "Do people still walk on the moon?"

"No," Mrs. O'Neill said. "There hasn't been a manned space voyage to the moon for decades."

"Why not?" J.P. asked.

Oliver could guess the answer: the moon

was too far away, was too cold, and didn't have enough gravity. And when you got there, it was just a bunch of rocks.

"Don't people want to study the moon's rocks?" J.P. continued.

Oliver knew that J.P. loved rocks. J.P.'s desk was full of rocks. Whenever Mrs. O'Neill had a desk-cleaning day, J.P. would drag out dozens of rocks from his desk, and Mrs. O'Neill would make him take them home. And then, Oliver knew, J.P.'s mother would make him put them outside in the backyard.

"I'm sure there are lots of scientists who would like to know more about the moon's rocks," Mrs. O'Neill said. "But recent manned space missions have stayed closer to Earth."

J.P. looked disappointed.

A girl named Sylvie Shi raised her hand. "Do animals ever go up into space?"

Oliver knew that by *animals* Sylvie meant *bunnies*. Sylvie had two bunnies of her own, and every time the class did an art project, Sylvie made hers a bunny. So far Sylvie had made a clay bunny, and a bunny puppet, and a silhouette bunny, and a bunny made out of papier-mâché.

"Some of the first creatures to go up into space were animals," Mrs. O'Neill replied. "The space scientists sent up a chimpanzee to make sure that it was safe before they sent up the first American astronaut, Alan Shepard."

"Didn't they care if it was safe for the chimp?" Sylvie demanded.

"I'm sure they did, Sylvie. And the chimp did survive the trip."

"What was the chimp's name?" Sylvie asked.

"His name was Ham," Mrs. O'Neill said. "Boys and girls, I'm glad you have so many good questions, and I hope we can answer them all over the next few weeks."

Oliver felt guilty. He didn't have any questions at all. He imagined his parents sitting at the dining room table trying to think of questions he could ask about space.

"Oliver, why don't you ask how cold it is on the moon?" his father would say.

"Oliver, why don't you ask how astronauts go to the bathroom in outer space?" his mother would say.

Oliver smothered a chuckle. His mother would never say that. She'd ask if there were seat belts in the rocket.

"Today I want to tell you a little bit about the early years of the space program," Mrs. O'Neill went on. "President John Fitzgerald Kennedy gave a famous speech on May 25, 1961. In that speech, he said, 'I believe that this nation should commit itself to achieving the goal, before this decade is out, of landing a man on the moon and returning him safely to the earth.' Until then no one had dreamed of putting a man on the moon. It seemed impossible."

Mrs. O'Neill paused. "But, boys and girls, it happened. Before the end of the decade, a man did walk on the moon."

She paused again. Oliver knew she was going to say something she thought was very important.

"One person with a big idea can change the world," Mrs. O'Neill said. "Maybe one of *you* will have an idea someday that will change the world."

Oliver stared at his desk. J.P. had big ideas about rocks. Sylvie had big ideas about bunnies. Crystal had big ideas about everything. Oliver wondered if he would ever have a big idea about anything.

"Now, when we finish our study of space," Mrs. O'Neill said, "we're going to have our space sleepover, right here in our classroom at school. This is the most exciting event of third grade! There will be all kinds of space activities, from looking through a real telescope at the stars and planets, to playing space games, to watching a science-fiction movie about adventures in outer space. I'll be sending the information to your parents next week."

"Can I bring my special meteorite rock for everyone to see?" J.P. asked.

"Can we bring stuffed animals with us?" Sylvie asked.

"Do we have to sleep, or can we stay up all night talking?" Crystal asked.

"Yes, yes, yes, and no," Mrs. O'Neill said with a smile.

Oliver tuned out. His parents would never let him go to the space sleepover. He might as well ask them if he could walk on the moon. Even President Kennedy wouldn't have been able to achieve the goal of landing Oliver at the space sleepover. J.P. had invited him for a sleepover half a dozen times, and Oliver's parents had always said no. Ever since he had been sickly as a little boy, and had waited a year to begin kindergarten, his parents, especially his mother, couldn't stop worrying about him.

Oliver looked up and scowled, as if it were somehow the moon's fault that he'd never get to see it through a real telescope. All he'd ever see was that stupid inflated ball, dangling from the classroom ceiling.

2

As part of their space study, all the kids in Oliver's class had to make a diorama of the solar system. They could work alone or with a friend.

Oliver was working with his parents.

Or, rather, Oliver was watching his parents work.

On Saturday morning, Oliver's father had three empty shoe boxes spread out on the dining room table: one small, one medium, one large.

Oliver's mother was reading aloud from the grading rubric on Mrs. O'Neill's assignment sheet. " 'Name on project—ten points.' George, make sure you put his name on it. The name is worth ten points!"

"Patsy, we'll put the name on last. How can I put the name on it when I don't even know which shoe box we're going to be using?"

Oliver thought he could put his own name on the project. *Oliver Olson*: 11 letters, 3 of them the same one, *o*. His parents probably could trust him to write his own name.

Oliver's mother continued reading. " 'All information about the solar system complete and accurate—fifty points.' What do you think she means by *complete*? How much information are you supposed to have in a diorama? George, what do you think?"

"How should I know?" Oliver's father asked. He was still studying the three shoe boxes. "Even this biggest one is too small, if the model is going to be to scale."

He turned to Oliver. "Oliver, go to the garage and get a bigger box."

"Oliver, go upstairs and get the solar system books we checked out of the library," his mother said at the same time.

Oliver sighed heavily.

He retrieved the library books first and gave them to his mother. He had read the shortest one last night.

In the garage, Oliver found the huge box from his father's new computer monitor, and the even huger box from his father's new computer. They were both too big for a diorama.

Oliver returned to the dining room empty-handed. "The boxes in the garage are too big."

"We need a big box!" His father sounded irritated. Building dioramas always made him irritated. "Go get the biggest one, the computer one."

" 'Attractiveness of the presentation—twenty points.' " Oliver's mother was still reading from the grading sheet. "What are we going to use to make the planets? Should we use Styrofoam balls? The rings of Saturn will be the hardest. Or the asteroid belt. How are we going to make the asteroid belt?"

Oliver brought the computer box into the dining room. He had seen a lot of dioramas in his day, but he had never seen one in a box big enough to hold a desktop computer and all its packing.

"Dioramas are supposed to be in shoe boxes," he told his dad as he set the computer box on the floor.

"Where does it say that? Patsy, read the directions again. What does it say about the size of the box?"

"'Originality—twenty points,'" Oliver's mother read.

Well, a diorama in a computer box would be original, Oliver supposed. So would a diorama in a refrigerator box, or a moving van.

"That's all it says," Oliver's mother told his father. "Name, ten points; accuracy, fifty points; attractiveness, twenty points; originality, twenty points. I still think it's ridiculous to give ten points for your name."

Oliver didn't think so. He thought it would be ridiculous to make a diorama inside a computer carton.

"Oliver, the box has to be big if the solar system is going to be built to scale." Oliver's father was using his patient, explaining-things voice. "Say the sun is as big as a tennis ball. Patsy, we have tennis balls around here somewhere, don't we? How far away would Earth have to be then?"

"About a mile?" Oliver guessed.

"Sarcasm isn't helpful, Oliver."

Oliver hadn't meant to be sarcastic. He opened the library book he had read to the page that showed the solar system to scale. "If the sun is as big as an *o* on one page, Earth is as big as a period on the other page."

His father slammed the book shut in disgust. "How does she expect us to make a diorama of the solar system to scale?"

Oliver didn't point out that Mrs. O'Neill wasn't expecting the parents to make anything at all. "I think we're just supposed to do the best we can," he offered.

"But accuracy is worth fifty points!" Now his mother sounded as upset as his father.

"I think she means things like getting the planets in the correct order, and putting rings on Saturn, and spelling their names right," Oliver said.

"Look," Oliver's father said, obviously trying to pull himself together. He set the computer

box on the dining room table. "Suppose we made the sun as big as a Ping-Pong ball. Then Earth would be as big as . . ."

"A pea?" Oliver suggested.

"How are we going to paint a pea so that it's attractive?" His mother's voice rose higher. "Attractiveness is worth twenty points. What's attractive about a pea?"

Not much, in Oliver's opinion.

"So, if the Ping-Pong ball is *here*"—Oliver's father pointed to the far side of the box—"where would the pea go?"

"In the kitchen?" Oliver asked.

"Oliver," his father said in a low, warning tone.

"It's not my fault that the solar system is big."

"All right." His father looked ready to concede defeat. "Suppose we don't make it to scale. The solar system is still going to look cramped in a shoe box."

That was okay, Oliver thought. When his parents made his diorama of the entire Amazon rain forest last year, it had looked cramped in a shoe box, too.

"I think we should use Styrofoam balls for the planets," his mother said. "We can paint Mars red. And we can put cotton around Venus, to be the cloud cover."

Oliver was getting bored listening to his parents talk about shoe boxes and Styrofoam balls. "I'm going over to J.P.'s house for a while," he said hopefully.

"Oliver!" his parents shouted together.

"This is *your* project," his father said.

"We need *you* to help," his mother said.

Oliver dropped into one of the dining room chairs, hidden from view behind the enormous computer box. It was going to be a long morning.

3

On Monday morning, right after math, Mrs. O'Neill wrote the names of the planets on the chalkboard: Mercury, Venus, Earth, Mars, Jupiter, Saturn, Uranus, Neptune. Oliver copied the list in his notebook, even though he already knew it from reading his library book. But the book included another planet, too, after Neptune—tiny, faraway Pluto.

"For years and years, I told my classes that there were nine planets," Mrs. O'Neill said, as if she had read Oliver's thoughts. "The eight I've put on the board, and Pluto. But now scientists have decided that Pluto shouldn't be counted as a planet. For one thing, Pluto is too small."

"J.P. is small," Crystal interrupted. J.P. was the shortest, skinniest boy in the class. "That doesn't mean he's not a person."

The rest of the class turned to inspect J.P. J.P. blushed. Oliver shot him a sympathetic look.

"My chihuahua is small," Crystal continued. "That doesn't mean she's not a dog. Rhode Island is small. That doesn't mean it's not a state."

"Crystal," Mrs. O'Neill said, "you didn't let me finish explaining. The scientists decided that if Pluto counted as a planet, lots of other things should count, as well. There are quite a few other bodies that orbit the sun and are even bigger than Pluto."

"Maybe they *should* count as planets," Crystal shot back. "I mean, who are these scientists?

Why do they get to decide what gets to be a planet and what doesn't? And all the scientists who thought Pluto was a planet—don't their views matter?"

"As scientists learn more, their views change," Mrs. O'Neill said. "At one time scientists thought the sun revolved around Earth. Now we know Earth revolves around the sun. Scientists are learning new things all the time."

"But that's a *fact*," Crystal said. "Either Earth revolves around the sun, or it doesn't. But Pluto being a planet or not—that's not a fact. That's more like, there's this club of planets, and Pluto got kicked out of the club."

Crystal was looking madder and madder. Oliver thought it was funny that someone would care so much about whether or not Pluto was a planet. But he found himself wanting to take Crystal's side. If Pluto had gotten to be a planet for all those years, why change things now? What harm would it do to let Pluto stay a

SPACE
ACTIVITIES

planet? Except that it would be one more Styrofoam ball he had to put in his computer-box diorama.

Sylvie was looking upset, too. "What if scientists just decide that some animals don't get to be animals anymore? Like—"

"Bunnies!" The rest of the class completed the sentence for her.

"Boys and girls," Mrs. O'Neill said, "I can tell we're going to want to learn more about Pluto. I'll find some articles to bring in to class that will give us a better explanation of how the scientific decision was made."

"Can we write to the scientists and tell them they're wrong?" Crystal asked.

Mrs. O'Neill smiled. "After you finish your planet work sheets, I'm going to tell you about an exciting opportunity for sharing lots of your good ideas. But now I need you to spend the next fifteen minutes on the planet assignment."

She passed a pile of work sheets around the room. Oliver saw that they were supposed to label the eight planets and color them and do a matching exercise about them. He already knew that "1. Largest planet" was "h. Jupiter" and "2. Planet with rings" was "d. Saturn."

"I'm going to add Pluto to mine," Crystal whispered to Oliver. She drew a small circle at the far left side of the page, pressing down hard with her pencil. "Plus, I'm going to put Pluto in my diorama."

Oliver had a thought. "You could put it outside the shoe box and make a little sign for it that says 'Let me in!' "

Crystal stared at Oliver. "That's wonderful! That's perfect! And we could have a petition for Pluto signed by the other planets. And we could have the scientists—we can cut out pictures of scientists from a magazine—we can have them with balloons coming out of their mouths, saying 'No!' We'll have the best diorama in the class."

It would be a great diorama, Oliver had to agree. But there was something about the way that Crystal kept saying "we" that was making him nervous.

"You'll do it with me, right?" Crystal asked.

What was he supposed to say? That his parents had already spent half of Saturday working on his diorama? That if he was going to work with somebody from school, he wanted to work with J.P.?

"Um . . . I've already gotten a lot done on mine." He *had* carried the computer box in from the garage. And he'd carried the library books downstairs from his bedroom.

"That's even better. That gives us a head start. Because it'll take time to find the scientist pictures and cut them out and glue them onto cardboard. Or we can make them like puppets, with Popsicle sticks on the back. Then we could act it out, for extra credit, maybe. We could do it as a skit at the space sleepover."

Before Oliver could say anything more, such as, What makes you think my parents are going to let me go to the space sleepover?, Crystal had her hand in the air. "Mrs. O'Neill, Oliver and I want to do our diorama together."

Mrs. O'Neill stopped by their desks. "That's fine. Have you finished your work sheets yet?" She looked down at Crystal's paper. All Crystal had done so far was add her drawing of Pluto. "Finish up, Crystal. And I'm looking forward to seeing what the two of you come up with."

Great. Oliver was *not* looking forward to telling his parents that his diorama was now going to be the first protest diorama in the history of the third grade.

"All right, third graders," Mrs. O'Neill told the class once all the planet work sheets had been turned in. "Who remembers what we learned the other day about big ideas?"

Crystal raised her hand.

"I see that Crystal remembers. Anyone else?"

Oliver remembered, but he didn't feel like raising his hand. To his surprise, Mrs. O'Neill called on him. "Oliver? I bet you remember."

"One person with a big idea can change the world," Oliver recited dutifully.

So far in his life he had had exactly one small idea, twenty minutes ago, and it wasn't going to change anything. It would only upset his parents, if he ever found the nerve to tell them. Maybe he would make two dioramas, one with them and one with Crystal. If Sylvie was the bunny kid, and J.P. was the rock kid, Oliver could be the diorama kid.

"Yes!" Mrs. O'Neill said. "Well, later this month our school is going to have a very special visitor, Colorado state senator Claire Levitt.

State senators work to pass laws to make our lives better, laws about education, highways, health care, and the environment. Senator Levitt will be speaking to the whole school at an assembly on the last Friday in April; your parents are invited to attend, too. That's the same day as our space sleepover, so it's going to be an exciting one for all of us."

Well, for some of us, Oliver thought.

Mrs. O'Neill paused in her favorite attention-getting way. "Boys and girls, I want each of you to come up with an idea that *you* think can change the world, and write that idea in a letter to Senator Levitt. I'll need it by Thursday of the week before she visits our school. Then I'll mail all of the ideas to her. Who knows? Maybe your idea will become a law."

"Does it have to be an idea about Colorado?" Crystal asked.

Oliver knew she was thinking about Pluto.

"No. Of course, an idea about Colorado is

more likely to become a law in Colorado. But your idea can be about anything you want. Anything in the world—or even out of it." She smiled at Crystal.

"All right, class, start thinking!"

4

The computer carton was still sitting
on Oliver's dining room table. Next to it lay an
enormous bag filled with Styrofoam balls of all
sizes, which Oliver's mother had bought at the
crafts store. The bag contained enough Styrofoam balls to make every planet and every moon
for every kid in Oliver's class.

Oliver reached inside the bag and pulled out
one of the smallest balls. "Hey, Pluto," he said to
it softly.

Oliver's mother was in the kitchen fixing him a healthy snack. He could hear her running water to wash away any trace of germs from his apple. He rolled his eyes, wondering if she had ever considered putting his apples through the dishwasher.

Oliver set Pluto on top of the carton. He imagined Pluto holding a tiny sign. He imagined what his parents would say when they saw the sign.

"Pluto," Oliver said, "we have a problem. I have to tell my mom I'm working with Crystal on the diorama."

Maybe if he practiced his speech to his mom right now, it would help.

"Okay, Pluto, pretend you're my mother."

It wasn't going to work. Pluto looked too small, too helpless, already defeated. Oliver fished around in the bag of Styrofoam balls and dug out the two biggest. They'd be good as the sun and Jupiter. For now the sun could be his father, and Jupiter could be his mother.

"Mom, Dad," Oliver said, addressing the two Styrofoam balls as they towered over Pluto on top of the carton, "there's something I need to tell you."

Jupiter and the sun waited for him to go on.

"Mrs. O'Neill said we have to work with partners on our diorama."

No. That was a lie, and his parents would find out it was a lie, and besides, he didn't want to lie.

"Mrs. O'Neill said we can work with partners on our diorama, and there's this girl, Crystal, and she asked me if I'd work with her."

That was all true.

"I hope you told her no," Oliver made Jupiter say.

"Well, actually, it's very hard to tell Crystal no." He'd like to see them try. "So I sort of told her yes."

Had he? As far as Oliver remembered, he

hadn't told Crystal anything. But she certainly assumed they were working together, and she had informed Mrs. O'Neill that they were.

"Anyway, I want to work with Crystal."

Did he? He was surprised at the answer: Yes, he did.

Oliver's mother came into the room bearing a plate with wedges of well-scrubbed organic apples, slices of low-fat cheese, and a brown rice cake.

"Who were you talking to, Oliver?" she asked.

"No one."

She looked worried.

"Just to myself."

She looked even more worried.

"I mean, I was thinking out loud about my diorama."

The worry lines in her forehead relaxed. "Here, have your snack. You washed your hands when you came home, right? I don't want you getting sick this spring the way you did last year when you had to miss all that school."

Oliver nodded. He took a bite of the rice cake. Maybe they could cut a hole in the middle of a rice cake and make it into a ring of Saturn.

"Mom," Oliver said. It might be easier to talk to her first, rather than to both of his parents together. On the other hand, he'd have to go through the speech twice, and it was going to be hard enough to go through it once.

"What is it, Oliver?"

He might as well just say it. "There's this girl in my class, and we want to do our diorama together."

The worry lines in his mother's forehead reappeared. "Oh, but, Oliver, remember when you did your science project with J.P. in second grade, and you had twenty points taken off for J.P.'s messy printing? What if your partner doesn't take it seriously?"

Crystal took the diorama seriously, all right.

But Crystal's idea of serious and his parents' idea of serious were completely different.

"What if she promises to do her part and she doesn't do it, and it's *your* grade that suffers?"

"She'll do her part."

"Which girl is it? What kind of student is she?"

"It's Crystal."

"Oh, Oliver. Isn't she the one who always gets into trouble for talking?"

"She has a lot to say."

"But—Oliver—your father—he's already put so much effort into this—selecting the box, worrying about the scale—"

"We'll use the computer box." Crystal would probably prefer a gigantic diorama. "And the Styrofoam balls, too." Oliver already thought of the Styrofoam balls as his friends.

To his amazement, Oliver sensed that his mother was weakening. If she had to convince

Oliver that working with Crystal was a bad idea, then she thought it was a real option.

"Well, we'll have to talk to your father when he gets home," she said. She sounded hurt and disappointed, but at least she hadn't come right out and told him no.

One down, one to go!

Inspired by this first success, or at least not complete failure, Oliver plunged ahead. "And, Mom? I want to go to the space sleepover."

Instantly she stiffened. "What space sleep-over?"

"The one at school. When we finish our study of outer space? Mrs. O'Neill sent home a sheet about it. We're going to sleep in sleeping bags and play games and look at the planets through a real telescope." He couldn't bear the idea that he would never see Jupiter's moons or Saturn's rings through an actual telescope. He just had to.

"Oliver, you and J.P. have asked us about sleepovers before, and you know the answer is no, and it's going to stay no."

"But everyone else is going."

"If everyone else jumped off a cliff, would you jump off, too?"

Oliver had heard that line before. "Going to a sleepover isn't like jumping off a cliff," he replied.

"Do you really think kids will sleep at this so-called sleepover? Do you think they will brush their teeth for two minutes before getting into their sleeping bags? Do you think they'll cover their mouths if they cough? Most of the other kids haven't had the health problems you've had. You know you always catch any sickness that's going around."

"Never mind," Oliver said. "I'd better go do my math homework."

He snatched Pluto from the top of the computer box, grabbed the phone, and stalked off to his room.

He shut the door and called J.P.

"My parents won't let me go to the space sleepover," he told J.P.

"I sort of didn't think they would," J.P. said. "I mean, your mom . . ."

"Are your parents letting you go?"

"Well, yeah, sure."

"Do you think there's anyone else in our class who won't be there?"

J.P. hesitated before he answered. "Um—no, not really."

Oliver said goodbye and hung up with a sigh.

Pluto would be the only planet not inside the space diorama. Oliver would be the only kid not going to the space sleepover.

He would never have guessed that he and Pluto had so much in common.

5

On Saturday morning, Oliver lugged his computer carton over to Crystal's house to begin working on their diorama together. In all his nine years of life, this was the most astonishing thing that had ever happened to him.

Oliver's father hadn't objected. Apparently he hated making dioramas more than Oliver or his mother had realized. That morning his dad looked like the sun himself, beaming as he got ready to go outside and tinker with the lawn mower instead of hanging Styrofoam balls inside a computer carton.

Oliver's mother had talked on the phone to Crystal's mother for ten minutes, asking the same questions she always asked before any playdate: Would an adult be in the house at all times? Were there any guns in the house? Would the kids be watching any violent programs on TV? Would they be using the Internet without supervision? She still asked J.P.'s mother these questions, even though Oliver went to J.P.'s house all the time. Fortunately, whatever answers Crystal's mother gave must have been the right ones.

So now Oliver and his carton and his sack of Styrofoam balls were all spending the morning with Crystal.

One of Crystal's dogs, the biggest one, jumped up onto Oliver and tried to lick his face.

Oliver's mother had forgotten to ask about badly trained dogs. J.P. didn't have any pets, only nice, quiet, well-behaved rocks.

"Down, Bart!" Crystal shouted.

Another, medium-sized dog, sniffed at Oliver's pants in an embarrassing place.

"Sit, Lisa!"

A tiny dog raced around Oliver, giving a series of high-pitched, excited barks.

"Quiet, Maggie!"

Oliver tried to hide his panic. There were so many dogs, and only one of him. They might bite, or slobber germs, or go to the bathroom on his leg. He stood as still as he could, barely breathing.

Finally Crystal succeeded in dragging or carrying all three dogs out of the room.

"How many dogs do you have?" Oliver asked, hoping his voice sounded normal.

"Just these three." Just! "Bart, Lisa, and Maggie, like the Simpsons."

Oliver must have looked blank.

"You know, the Simpsons? The cartoon on TV?"

"I'm not allowed to watch cartoons," Oliver confessed.

Crystal's jaw dropped. "You don't have any dogs, either, do you? I can tell."

"I don't have any pets."

"Why not?"

"They have germs, and they shed, and they damage the furniture." Oliver recited his mother's reasons.

"So? They also love you and act thrilled whenever they see you and sleep in your bed."

Oliver shuddered. He would not want dogs like Crystal's sleeping next to him in his neatly made bed. If any dog tried to sleep in any bed in his house, his mother would die. She would literally keel over with horror, and that would be the end of her.

"I think we'd better get started on the diorama," Oliver said in a strangled voice.

"Okay. Why don't you pick out the planets and figure out how to hang them in the box. I'll go through these magazines and look for pictures of scientists."

It wasn't hard selecting the planets, especially since Oliver had already picked out the sun, Jupiter, and Pluto. "How should we hang them in the box?" he asked.

Crystal shrugged. "The garage is full of stuff we can use." She pointed toward a door that led off the kitchen.

"Are there . . . The dogs won't be in the garage, will they?"

"No." Crystal laughed. "But you'll find everything else you can imagine."

There were no cars in the garage, either, it turned out. The garage was completely filled with bicycles, boards, bricks, broken pieces of furniture, and piles of odd rubbish. Oliver didn't know what he should be looking for. Wire? String? And where should he be looking? He was relieved when, on a shelf against one wall, he found a ball of twine and a long piece of thin wire.

Returning to the kitchen, Oliver saw that Crystal had given up on her stack of magazines and was drawing scientists on pieces of cardboard.

"Which do you think is better, wire or string?" Oliver asked.

"Wire," Crystal said without looking up from her drawing.

"Um . . . what do I cut it with?"

"There are some pliers in the toolbox on the table in the garage."

Back in the garage again, Oliver found the toolbox, filled with a jumble of tools. He recognized hammers, but all the rest looked equally mysterious. If only one had been labeled "pliers—good for cutting wire." He dragged the heavy box from the garage to the kitchen.

"Um . . . what do pliers look like?"

Crystal reached into the toolbox and plucked them out and handed them to Oliver.

He hated to bother her again, but he had no choice. "Um . . . how do you use them?"

He expected Crystal to give a snort of disgust, but she just picked up the pliers and showed him how to snip off a piece of wire.

Now he wanted to ask her how long the pieces of wire should be, but instead he studied the size of the carton. Carefully he snipped off nine pieces of wire, one for each of the planets, not counting Pluto, and one for the sun. Ta-da!

"We need to paint the planets first," he told Crystal. "Do you have any paint?"

Forty-five minutes later, Oliver had painted all the planets. At first he felt nervous painting without a smock to cover his clothes, but he hadn't seen any smocks in the garage. No dogs, no cars, no smocks.

When he had finished, Oliver lined up the planets in a row on the kitchen table to dry. He stood back to gaze in admiration at his work. He was especially impressed with the orange and white bands he had painted on Jupiter and the dark sunspots he had painted on the sun. Of course, he'd be able to paint them even better if he could see them through a real telescope.

"How do you think the planets look?" he asked Crystal, fishing for a compliment.

Crystal studied them. "Beautiful!"

Just then Crystal's older brother came into the kitchen. Unfortunately, three high-spirited dogs came bounding in with him.

Before Oliver knew what was happening, Bart was jumping up onto him, washing Oliver's face with his tongue. Maggie was barking and sniffing at Oliver's ankles. Worst of all, Lisa pounced on the row of expertly painted, proudly drying planets. Before Oliver's very eyes, the smallest planet was carried away in her mouth.

Pluto!

All that Oliver could do was to paint a second Pluto. At his neat, orderly house, Pluto would have had a safer life—but at his house, his parents would have made the diorama for him, and Pluto wouldn't have gotten to be in it at all.

Oliver felt bad for the first Pluto, though. Death by dog chewing was a tragic way to go.

6

Jupiter had at least sixty-three moons that revolved around it, Mrs. O'Neill told Oliver's class that Wednesday. It had so many moons that some of them didn't even have names.

"We could give them names," Crystal suggested.

"What do you think would be a good name for a moon?" Mrs. O'Neill asked.

Lots of hands shot into the air. Kids wanted to name moons after themselves, after their pets, and after characters from cartoons that Oliver had never seen.

Oliver didn't raise his hand. Any name would be better than the name of Earth's own moon: Moon. That was like naming your dog Dog or your cat Cat. It was practically the same as not having a name at all.

"Can we send the names to Senator Levitt?" Crystal asked.

"We should probably send them to NASA," Mrs. O'Neill said. "But we can send them to Senator Levitt, too. I hope you have started thinking of some world-changing ideas to send her."

Oliver didn't have any so far. He hadn't told his parents about the assignment yet.

"Scientists know a lot about Jupiter's largest moons," Mrs. O'Neill said. "Those moons got their names from characters in Greek mythology. The moon Io has many volcanoes. The moon Europa has water on it, just like Earth."

"Can you swim in it?" Sylvie asked.

"It's all frozen," Mrs. O'Neill said, "because Jupiter is so far away from the sun and so cold. Another moon, Ganymede, is even larger than the planet Mercury."

That meant it was larger than Pluto, too.

Mrs. O'Neill told the class that the four largest planets—Jupiter, Saturn, Uranus, and Neptune—weren't hard and rocky like Mercury, Venus, Earth, and Mars. "They are largely made of gas," she said. "They are called the gas giants."

"Can you walk on them?" J.P. asked.

Mrs. O'Neill shook her head. "No. I don't think people will ever walk on them the way we walked on the moon."

Oliver thought about Neil Armstrong walking on the moon. It would be strange to do something you knew would be in history books forever. Kids in school would learn about you for centuries. You would be an answer to a matching question:

8. First man to walk on the moon
d. Neil Armstrong

Maybe Crystal would grow up to be the answer to a matching question:

4. Pluto protester
k. Crystal Harding

"Jupiter is one of the few planets you can see with the naked eye," Mrs. O'Neill went on.

Some kids laughed at the word *naked*.

"Jupiter is not as bright as Venus, but it's

bright enough to see on a clear night. At the space sleepover, you'll get an even better look at Jupiter through the telescope."

Oliver had a thought: his parents might let him come for the first part of the sleepover—the non-sleeping part. That way he could see Jupiter through a telescope and check out its colored bands and Great Red Spot. But it would be embarrassing and pitiful when his parents came to pick him up just as J.P. and everyone else were zipping into their sleeping bags to watch *Star Wars*. It would be even worse than not going to the sleepover at all.

Mrs. O'Neill put a CD into the class CD player. "Boys and girls, now I'm going to play you a piece of music about Jupiter by the composer Gustav Holst. As you listen, see if the music makes you think of a large, majestic planet, the king of all the planets, moving slowly across the night sky."

Oliver closed his eyes to listen. The music

did remind him of something great and powerful.

If there was music for Pluto, what would it sound like? A tiny whimper, maybe, that nobody except Oliver could hear.

After school, Oliver's mother had a protein bar for him, with carrot sticks and a glass of tomato juice. Oliver imagined astronauts eating the bar in outer space: a day's worth of calories and nutrients squeezed into a dark, dense cube. There was going to be pizza at the space sleepover.

"What do you have for homework?" his mother asked.

"Just some math and spelling. Oh, and we have to think of an idea that could change the world."

It was a pretty ridiculous assignment, when you thought about it. Oliver explained to his mother about Senator Levitt's visit.

"Mrs. O'Neill told us it could be any kind of

idea, really," Oliver said. "Like for a new law in Colorado."

"I have the perfect idea!" his mother said. Oliver started to feel nervous.

"Have you noticed how many parents make U-turns in front of the school after they drop off their children in the morning?"

Oliver couldn't say that he had.

"One of these days there's going to be an accident there. So your idea could be to put a sign by the school that says NO U-TURNS."

"That would be my world-changing idea?"

"It could save someone's life!" Oliver's mother sounded defensive now. "It could change the world for one person at least."

Oliver took a sip of tomato juice to wash down his bite of protein bar.

"Well, go do your math and spelling so I can check them before dinner. We can work on your idea for Senator Levitt when your father gets home. You want to come up with an idea for something that a state senator could actually accomplish."

Oliver took another gulp of juice. "Mrs. O'Neill said there's going to be a telescope at the space sleepover. We'll be able to see Jupiter. Doesn't that sound educational?"

And wonderful? he wanted to add.

His mother could hardly deny it. "Yes, but . . . I suppose you could go to that part and come home before bedtime."

Oliver had known that was what she'd say.

"No one else will be going home early," he said pleadingly.

He hoped she wouldn't get teary-eyed and start talking about how sick he had been when he was four.

"Oliver, we've already discussed this, and the answer is still no."

Oliver felt the stirring of a world-changing idea. There should be a law that all kids were allowed to attend all school activities, especially sleepovers.

Or that parents were required to listen—really listen—to what their children wanted to do.

Or that protein bars should be banned forever.

He looked down at the rest of his protein bar, lying leaden on his plate like the largest, heaviest moon of Jupiter.

Where were Crystal's dogs when he needed them?

7

The next Saturday, Crystal's father drove Crystal and the diorama to Oliver's house. Oliver was nervous.

What would his parents think about Crystal?

What would Crystal think about his parents?

At first everything seemed all right. Oliver's mother covered the dining room table with old newspapers. Crystal set the diorama in the middle of it.

"Is there anything you two need?" Oliver's mother asked.

"No thanks, Mrs. Olson," Crystal said politely.

"A snack?"

Oliver gave Crystal a quick shake of his head while his mother wasn't looking.

"We're fine," she said.

"Let me see how the diorama is coming along."

Oliver groaned to himself. His mother peered into the cavernous computer box, where his neatly painted Styrofoam balls hung on their wires. So far it looked like a normal diorama.

"Don't you think Jupiter and Saturn are too close together?" his mother asked. "Could you move them so they're not touching?"

Oliver waited to see what Crystal would say. The whole time at Crystal's house, her parents hadn't made any comments whatsoever about their work. The only family members who had taken any interest in the project had been Crystal's dogs.

"Sure." Crystal smiled agreeably at Oliver's mother.

Then Oliver's mother picked up the sheet of planet facts Crystal had printed neatly: the name of every planet, its color, its gravity, its moons.

"Crystal dear, did you do all this?" she asked. "It looks very nice. I did notice a few errors here and there. Is it all right if I go ahead and mark them?"

"Sure," Crystal repeated. This time she didn't smile.

"It's just that accuracy is worth fifty percent of your grade," Oliver's mother explained. She picked up a pencil and began lightly circling some misspellings.

"Also . . . don't you think it would add something if you explained how each planet got its name? The names come from Greek and Ro-

man mythology, you know: Venus, the goddess of love; Mars, the god of war."

For the first time since Oliver had known her, Crystal had nothing to say. After a long pause, she replied, "Well, we have some other stuff we want to add instead."

Oliver hoped she wasn't going to tell his mother about Pluto and the "Let me in!" sign and the hostile scientists. But she seemed to be figuring things out on her own.

"Mom, we have a lot to do," Oliver said.

"All right, honey," his mother said. Oliver could tell that her feelings were hurt. "But if you need anything, let me know."

When she left, Oliver's stomach unclenched with relief.

Crystal stared after her. "Is your mother always—you know—like this?" She reached inside the diorama and moved Saturn's wire so that Saturn was farther away from Jupiter.

Oliver nodded miserably. "She worries a lot

about my grades," he said, as if it weren't obvious. "It's because I had to wait a year to go to kindergarten, so I guess she thinks I'm always behind in everything."

"Wow," Crystal said sympathetically.

Oliver felt himself flushing with embarrassment, which turned to anger, not at Crystal, but at his mother. "I think . . ." he began. "I think schools should make a rule that parents *can't* help with homework. It's like—what's the *point* of homework if the parents do it?"

"Oliver," Crystal said solemnly, "that is a *great* idea. That can be your idea to send to Senator Levitt! Go ahead, write it down before you forget." She shoved a sheet of paper at him.

Oliver thought it was a pretty terrific idea, too, even better than the ban on protein bars. But then he said, "I can't send it. My mother already thought up an idea she wants me to use." He told Crystal his mother's suggestion.

"U-turns?!" Crystal's voice was almost a

shriek. "Oliver, your idea is ten thousand times better. At least write it down. You write it down while I paint the outside of the carton. What color do you think we should make it? Maybe dark blue? Sort of like the night sky?"

For the next few minutes, Oliver wrote while Crystal painted.

Then his mother reappeared in the dining room.

"Oh, Crystal, wait, let me get you one of Oliver's smocks. You'll get paint all over that pretty top."

A moment later, Oliver's mother had tied a smock around Crystal's neck. She tied one on Oliver, too.

Then she peeked into the diorama. "You did move Saturn!" She glanced toward Oliver's paper. He tried to cover it with his arm without making it look as if he was trying to cover it with his arm.

"I'm glad you're working on more information to add," his mother said. "All right, I'll go
now. Let me know when you're ready for a
snack."

When they were alone again, Oliver quickly
finished writing his idea.

"Give it to me," Crystal said. She took his
paper and tucked it into her science notebook.
"I'll keep it at my house, in case you change
your mind and want to send it in to Senator
Levitt. Maybe we should make the sign for Pluto
and glue on all the scientists at my house, too."

Oliver looked at Pluto number two, sitting
alone on the paint-streaked newspaper. "Yeah,"
he said.

Oliver took a turn with the paintbrush. The
computer carton looked a lot better now, with its
coat of midnight blue.

"Are we going to paint the inside?" he asked.

"We should. But we'll have to take the planets out, or else be really careful not to get paint on them. Your mother doesn't have teensy-weensy smocks, does she?"

Oliver laughed.

His mother came into the dining room as he and Crystal were putting the planets back into the freshly painted interior of the carton. Oliver was impressed that she had made herself stay away for an entire twenty minutes.

"Much better!" she praised. "Maybe add some of these shiny stick-on stars in the background? So it won't look so dark?"

As she spoke, she picked up the paint-covered newspapers to put in the trash. "Now let me bring you that snack."

Only after she had bustled away with the crumpled papers did Oliver realize that a small Styrofoam ball had been swept along with them: Pluto number two. Even at his neat, orderly house, apparently, Pluto wasn't safe from destruction.

Oliver broke the news to Crystal. "She threw away Pluto."

Crystal burst out laughing. She handed Oliver the bag of Styrofoam balls. "Okay," she said. "Pick out Pluto number three."

8

Mrs. O'Neill always kept her promises. On Thursday, the same day their world-changing ideas were due, she brought to class a folder filled with articles about Pluto.

"Is Pluto a planet?" she wrote on the chalkboard.

The main problem with Pluto, she explained, wasn't so much that Pluto was small but that its orbit was irregular, and it wasn't significantly bigger than its own moon, Charon.

"The scientists said that a planet needs to 'dominate its neighborhood.' All the other planets are much bigger than their moons. But Pluto isn't."

Oliver could see Crystal ready to explode with indignation. J.P. was looking at her, too. The boys exchanged grins.

Mrs. O'Neill smiled. "Yes, Crystal?"

"That makes it sound like a real planet has to be some kind of bully! Like it has to be able to beat up all its moons."

"I don't think that's what the scientists meant," Mrs. O'Neill said. "According to them, if Pluto counts as a planet, then dozens of other objects, like dwarf planets Ceres and Eris, should also be counted."

"Maybe they *should* be counted!" Crystal said. "Or maybe . . . maybe Pluto's special, just because it already got to be a planet for so long."

Mrs. O'Neill looked thoughtful. "Actually,

some astronomers agree with you, Crystal. They think Pluto should still be considered a planet for historical and cultural reasons— because we are so used to thinking of Pluto that way."

"Isn't that a good reason?" Crystal demanded.

"I don't know," Mrs. O'Neill replied. "What do you think? *Is* that a good reason for doing something? Because we've always done it that way before?"

Now Crystal looked uncertain. Oliver felt uncertain, too. His parents had always done his dioramas for him; this time he was doing his own diorama. His parents had never let him go to a sleepover; now he wanted to go to one more than anything in the world. He didn't want to keep on doing things for the rest of his life the same way he had always done them.

Crystal hesitated. Then she said, "I think it depends. On what kind of thing it is."

Mrs. O'Neill smiled again. "That's an excellent answer, Crystal."

The class talked more about Pluto, with lots of kids for Pluto being a planet, including Crystal, Oliver, and Sylvie, and lots of kids against, including J.P. In the end, Mrs. O'Neill let the class vote. Pluto won, but it was close: 14–12.

"Now," Mrs. O'Neill said, "I want you all to share your world-changing ideas before you hand them in. After school today I'm going to mail them to Senator Levitt."

Oliver hoped he wouldn't have to read his, but Mrs. O'Neill said, "We'll just go around the room in order," and he knew then that he wasn't going to be able to avoid it.

The boy in the first seat, Scott Healy, read, "My idea is to make jet-powered skateboards that will go really fast."

Then Angie Fettig read, "My idea is to give food to hungry people so that they don't die, and if they do die, to go to their funerals."

Tony Mungo's idea was to build robots that could do homework for kids. The class cheered at that one. James Alpert wanted to fire special ice pellets into space to cool off the atmosphere and stop global warming. Melanie Sparks thought the government should pay for hospitals for poor people.

Sylvie read hers: "I heard that people test eye makeup on bunnies' eyes. I think that's really wrong, and there should be a law against it. People shouldn't wear eye makeup, anyway, and if they want to wear it, they should test it on their own eyes."

J.P. read his: "I think the government should give more money for research on rocks. Rocks are very interesting, and people should find out more about them." Oliver shot him a grin.

Crystal had lots of ideas, including letting Pluto be a planet again. Mrs. O'Neill told her to pick just one idea to share, so she read: "I would make a law that kids can't get into trouble for talking in class. Some people are naturally talkative, and some people are naturally quiet, and it isn't fair that the naturally talkative people should have their desks moved all the time."

Lots of kids laughed, and Mrs. O'Neill said, "I'll be sure to give your idea careful consideration, Crystal."

Now it was Oliver's turn. He kept his voice dull and read without expression; he wasn't even going to pretend that he was excited about U-turns.

"Many parents make U-turns in front of the school when they drop their kids off in the morning. This is unsafe and could cause an accident. My idea is to put up a sign in front of the school that says NO U-TURNS."

He wondered if Mrs. O'Neill would comment on his idea. She just looked at him with a question in her eyes. Then she went on to a kid who wanted a law that movie theaters couldn't charge so much for their popcorn.

When everybody had finished, Mrs. O'Neill said, "If some of these ideas were adopted, I think the world would be a much better place. Now we'll see what Senator Levitt thinks. She'll be at our school assembly a week from tomorrow, the day of our third-grade space sleepover!"

The space sleepover with the entire third grade, except for Oliver.

Oliver and Crystal finished their diorama on Saturday morning, at Crystal's house. This time her mother took the dogs on a long walk, so nothing happened to Pluto number three. He looked cute, perched on top of the enormous carton, with his small sign crying, "Let me in!"—one little planet against all the cardboard cutout scientists with their sneering faces and unfriendly scowls.

"It looks great," Oliver told Crystal.

"It does," she agreed.

She was quiet for a moment. Then she said, "But you know what, Oliver? I've changed my mind. I *don't* think Pluto should be a planet."

Oliver was stunned.

"I think the scientists are right," Crystal said slowly. "If dozens of other things are just as big as Pluto, and orbit the sun just like Pluto, then it isn't fair to make Pluto a planet just because the scientists found out about Pluto first."

Deep inside, Oliver found himself agreeing with Crystal. He didn't want people to keep on doing something just because it was the way they had always done it.

Then he was alarmed. "We don't have to do the diorama over again, do we?"

Crystal patted him on the shoulder. "No. Somebody needed to stand up for Pluto, and we did it. But—there wouldn't be any world-changing ideas if everybody kept on thinking the same way forever. There wouldn't be any reason to write to Senator Levitt if nothing was ever going to change."

Oliver watched as Crystal picked up Pluto number three and gave him a small, sad kiss. "You're not a planet," she whispered. Then she set him back gently on top of the diorama.

9

"Did you get your grade on your diorama yet?" Oliver's mother asked him after school on Thursday as she brought him his snack.

"Uh-huh," Oliver responded casually. He took a bite of his protein bar and chewed it slowly. There was no way to chew one of his mother's protein bars quickly.

"Oliver, why didn't you tell me right away?"

Oliver shrugged. He tried to keep his face from showing any expression.

"Oh, Oliver, did you get a B? I knew it was a mistake for you to work with that girl. Why didn't the two of you add that information about the planet names, the way I asked you to?"

She sounded so upset that Oliver couldn't tease her any longer. Still chewing, he got up and fished out the grading sheet from his backpack. He watched her face as he handed it to her.

"A plus?! One hundred percent? Oliver, why *didn't* you tell me? This is wonderful!"

Oliver couldn't keep from grinning.

"But wait . . ." Her brow creased as she continued reading down the grade sheet. "You lost ten points for not remembering to put on your names. And those were the easiest ten points to get!"

"But we got an extra ten points, extra credit,

for creativity and originality," Oliver said. "So we got a hundred, anyway."

And the most creative and original part—the whole plan of putting Pluto outside the diorama with the protest sign—had been his idea. Senator Levitt might never know about his real world-changing idea, but at least he had gotten an A+ for his diorama-changing idea.

Oliver's mother gave him a hug. "I can't wait to see it!"

"You can see it tomorrow," Oliver promised, "after the assembly."

He was just glad that she had seen the grade first.

The all-purpose room was unusually crowded on Friday afternoon. In addition to the whole school sitting cross-legged on the cold, bare floor, rows of folding chairs had been set up in the back for parents who wanted to hear Senator Levitt speak. Both of Oliver's parents were there. His mom didn't work, so she always came to everything. His dad had taken off the afternoon from his job at the insurance company.

Senator Levitt looked different from what Oliver had expected. She was tiny, shorter than some of the fifth graders.

Oliver imagined Crystal saying, Senator Levitt's small, but she's still a senator.

The senator wore a bright red suit. That surprised Oliver, too, that a senator would be so colorful.

First the students all stood up and said the Pledge of Allegiance, even though they had said it that morning. Then the fifth graders sang "It's a Grand Old Flag." Senator Levitt clapped enthusiastically.

When it was her turn at the microphone, Senator Levitt began by saying what an honor it was to be a state senator. She spoke about some of the problems that the state of Colorado faced, which she and her fellow senators were trying to solve: crowded highways, air pollution, insufficient funding for public schools.

The kindergartners began squirming, then the first graders.

J.P. whispered to Oliver, "Colorado has too many problems."

Oliver grinned. He had too many problems, too.

One first grader poked another first grader and was made to sit by himself right in front of his teacher. J.P. yawned, and Oliver couldn't help joining in.

"In closing . . ." Senator Levitt said—Oliver could feel the audience perk up again—"I want to tell you children how impressed I am by the interesting ideas one class sent me to help me represent you better. Which class sent me their ideas for changing the world? Will you please stand up so I can see who you are?"

The kids in Oliver's class scrambled to their

feet. The rest of the school applauded, probably grateful for something to do. Oliver's class plopped down onto the floor again.

"Most of your suggestions are beyond what we can tackle in the state legislature. We don't shape national policy—that's done in Washington. And we don't deal with local school policy—that's done right here in your own school district. So I hope you'll share some of your thoughts with your U.S. senators and with your principal."

Oliver guessed his mother would make him send the U-turn idea to the principal.

"But since I'm here at the microphone, and your principal and teachers and parents are here, too, I'd like to mention a few of the ideas I think are especially worth sharing. Sylvie Shi had an excellent suggestion about not testing new products on animals. Angie Fettig and Melanie Sparks both remind us about the importance of helping the needy. But my favorite idea was the one sent in by a young man named Oliver Olson."

Oliver almost fainted. If he had been sitting in one of the folding chairs, he would have fallen out of it onto the floor. Was his mother right, after all, and a NO U-TURNS sign was more exciting than riding a jet-powered skateboard or ending world hunger or finding a new way to stop global warming? J.P. shook his head in disbelief.

Oliver knew the rest of his classmates were staring at him, so he gazed down at his shoes. One lace was dragging on the floor. He was surprised that his mother hadn't hurried forward to tie it for him.

"Oliver Olson suggested a school policy that parents not be allowed to help with homework."

Oliver's whole body tensed with shock. Crystal crowed, "I sent it in! I knew it was a great idea, so I sent it in myself!"

"Crystal!" Mrs. O'Neill whispered warningly from her chair a few feet away. She put her finger to her lips. But she didn't look angry.

Senator Levitt continued, "Oliver wrote that when parents help with homework, it isn't fair to the students who have to do their own work without any help. And it isn't fair to the students who get the extra help, either, because they don't learn as much. Oliver Olson, are you here this afternoon?"

He couldn't very well hide, with Crystal and J.P. both shouting out, "Here he is!"

This time Oliver stood up all by himself. The rest of the school clapped even louder than before.

Senator Levitt smiled at him. Oliver found himself smiling back.

"Congratulations, Oliver. And thanks to all of you for being such a wonderful audience," Senator Levitt said.

The second graders sang "America the Beautiful," and the assembly was over.

Now all Oliver had to do was go back to his classroom and face his parents. For the first time, he envied tiny, distant Pluto, a safe three billion miles away.

10

Oliver knew he'd see his parents in his classroom; Mrs. O'Neill had sent home a note inviting parents who were attending the assembly to come admire the display of dioramas afterward.

Right behind him in line, as they walked back to the room, Crystal kept on talking. But Oliver wasn't listening. He didn't want his parents to be angry. Even more, he didn't want his parents, especially his mother, to be sad.

There they were, standing together in front of the computer carton, the largest diorama by far. Quietly Oliver slipped behind them.

His mother whirled around. "Oliver!" She grabbed him into a hug. "When Senator Levitt said your name, we were so proud! We should have brought the video camera!"

Oliver almost felt like crying from relief.

Shaking his head in disbelief, Oliver's father picked up Pluto. " 'Let me in!' " he quoted with a chuckle. "How did you two think up this stuff?"

Oliver shrugged modestly, as if he had so many dazzling ideas he hardly remembered how he came to each one.

"But, Oliver," his mother began, "was that really your idea, about the homework? What happened to the idea about the U-turns?"

"Both of them got sent in." It was too complicated to explain.

His mother looked worried. "I'm sure there

are some parents who help their children too much," she said, "and your father and I do help you all we can, but—do you think *we* help too much?"

He might as well say it. "Kind of."

"With homework?"

"Well, with everything."

Even as he said it, his mother looked down and saw his dangling shoelace. "Oliver, your shoe! You'll trip if you have it dragging along on the floor like that." She knelt down and tied it snugly with a double knot.

When she stood up again, Oliver and his father were both grinning.

"What?" she asked. "Oh." She flushed. "But you'll *fall* if you walk around with your shoelaces untied. You could break a bone!"

"Which is why Oliver should learn to tie his shoes for himself," his father said.

Crystal danced up next to them. "Go, Oliver!" she cheered. "That was pretty cool, with Senator Levitt, wasn't it?" she asked Oliver's parents.

"It certainly was," Oliver's mother said with a strained smile.

"You came up with a pretty wild idea for a diorama," Oliver's father told her.

"Oh, that was Oliver's idea," Crystal said. His parents were looking more and more bewildered. "But I drew the scientists."

Mrs. O'Neill joined the group. "Congratulations, Oliver! Maybe, with your good ideas, you'll be a senator someday, giving a speech right here at this very school."

Oliver hoped not. He wouldn't mind being a senator, but he didn't want to give a speech at the school. He didn't want to bore so many kids sitting for so long on such a hard floor.

There was something he did want, though, and this was the best chance he would ever have to get it.

"Mom? Dad? I want to go to the space sleepover tonight."

"Oliver," his mother said in a low, warning tone.

But Oliver forged ahead. Nothing was going to stop him now. "Mom, I got an A plus on my diorama, using *my* idea. Senator Levitt read *my* idea out loud to the whole assembly. You don't need to do everything for me forever. What if Neil Armstrong's mom hadn't let him walk on the moon? What if John F. Kennedy's mom hadn't let him run for President? What if Senator Levitt's mom hadn't let her run for state senator?" He tried to think of more examples, but maybe he had already said enough.

Oliver's dad cleared his throat. "Aw, let him go, Patsy."

Mrs. O'Neill hesitated; then she said, "There will be plenty of parental supervision. We're going to take very good care of them, Mrs. Olson."

For once Crystal didn't say anything, but begging was written all over her face.

"Oh, Oliver," his mother said. Oliver saw that she had tears in her eyes. "But you won't drink any soda, will you? And you'll brush your teeth for two minutes, the same way you would at home? And you'll tell Mrs. O'Neill right away if you aren't feeling well?"

This time Oliver reached out and hugged her. "I will," he said. He was ready to promise her the sun, the moon, Mercury, Venus, Earth, Mars, Jupiter, Saturn, Uranus, Neptune, and especially Pluto, if she wanted.

He was going to the space sleepover!

Oliver's favorite activity at the space sleepover was going outside into the April darkness and looking at the sky through the telescope. He could see the same colored bands on Jupiter that he had tried to paint on his Styrofoam ball. It was like seeing his diorama come to life before his very eyes. He could hear in his head the grand, soaring music Mrs. O'Neill had played for the class.

The sky was studded with stars in bright, twinkling patterns. Oliver couldn't recognize any constellations. His class hadn't studied the stars this year, only planets. But Oliver knew he'd study stars someday. Maybe he'd read all he could about astronomy and grow up to be a famous astronomer.

9. Who was the   e. Oliver Olson!
most famous
astronomer of the
early twenty-first
century?

Oliver's least favorite activity at the space sleepover was going inside an inflated room set up in the gym, where everyone bounced up and down pretending it had less gravity than Earth.

There were too many kids bouncing at once, and shouting, and pushing each other. At least Oliver could say that he had done it, though.

Then Oliver wondered what he and J.P. would do at their first sleepover. And at the sleepover after that.

When it was time to brush teeth and get ready for bed, Oliver walked with his toothbrush and toothpaste past his diorama to say good night to Pluto.

Pluto was gone.

Oliver looked inside the diorama, thinking maybe one of his classmates had decided to let Pluto in, after all. He looked on the floor underneath the diorama table. He looked inside the other, much smaller, dioramas on the table.

No Pluto.

Toothbrush and toothpaste still in hand, Oliver went to find Crystal. She was talking to a group of girls who were already tucked into their sleeping bags with their stuffed animals.

Sylvie, Oliver saw, had a whole family of plush bunnies with her.

"Crystal," Oliver interrupted, "I need to talk to you for a minute."

He led her to the diorama. "Pluto's gone. I've looked everywhere, but he's disappeared."

"I bet I know where he is." Crystal lowered her voice. "I think Sylvie's little sister took him. I saw her playing with him the whole time their parents were dropping Sylvie off for the sleep-over."

Oliver did remember a small girl with dark pigtails lingering by the dioramas.

"It's okay," Crystal told him. "She'll give him a good home."

Oliver said a silent farewell to Pluto number three. Maybe this was the ultimate proof that Pluto wasn't meant to be a planet, after all.

Ten minutes later, Oliver was snug in his own sleeping bag, next to J.P.'s. His teeth were extremely well brushed; his mother would have been proud. He hadn't brought a stuffed animal to the sleepover, though. It was enough that he had brought himself.

Mrs. O'Neill turned down the lights to show the *Star Wars* movie. Oliver could still see the dim shapes of the planets hung from the ceiling in their classroom.

Perfectly content, Oliver lay there and smiled up at the moon.

Fun Facts about Pluto

- Pluto was considered to be a planet for only seventy-six years, from when it was discovered in 1930 until when it was demoted to a dwarf planet in 2006.

- Pluto is smaller than Earth's moon.

- Pluto's largest moon, Charon, is half as big as Pluto.

- Pluto's diameter is only about half the length of the United States.

- One year on Pluto (the time it takes Pluto to orbit the sun) equals about 248 Earth years.

- One day on Pluto (the time it takes for Pluto to turn on its axis) is equivalent in Earth days to six days, nine hours, and seventeen minutes.

- Pluto's average temperature is about -375 degrees Fahrenheit (-226 degrees Celsius).

- A person who weighs one hundred pounds (forty-five kilograms) on Earth would weigh only seven pounds (three kilograms) on Pluto.

- Pluto is the only planet to be named by a kid! Eleven-year-old Venetia Burney of Oxford, England, suggested that dark, cold, faraway Pluto should be named after the Roman god of the underworld.

- The first spacecraft ever to travel to Pluto, New Horizons, is scheduled to reach Pluto in 2015 (don't worry, no humans aboard).

GO FISH

CLAUDIA MILLS

Larry Harwood

What did you want to be when you grew up?
I always wanted to be a writer. The only other thing I even considered being was president of the United States. In third grade, I made a hundred-dollar bet with Jimmy Burnett that I would be president someday, but now I'm starting to think maybe Jimmy Burnett is going to win that bet.

When did you realize you wanted to be a writer?
When I was six and my sister was five, my mother gave each of us one of those marble composition notebooks. She told me that my notebook was supposed to be my poetry book, and she told my sister that her notebook was supposed to be her journal. So I started writing poetry, and my sister started keeping a journal, and we both found out that we loved doing it.

What's your most embarrassing childhood memory?

Oh, there are so many! One day in third grade, I decided to run away from school, and I made a very public announcement to that effect. But when I got to the edge of the playground, I realized I had no place to go, so I had to come slinking back again. That memory still makes me cringe.

What's your favorite childhood memory?

We vacationed every summer at a little lake in New Hampshire, and I remember sitting out on the lake in a rowboat, writing poems and drawing pictures and making up stories about imaginary princesses with my sister. Those were very happy days.

As a young person, who did you look up to most?

I mostly looked up to characters in books who were braver and stronger than I was, like Sara Crewe in *A Little Princess,* who loses her beloved father and has to live in poverty in Miss Minchin's cold, miserable garret, but never stops acting like the princess that she feels she is in inside. I also looked up to Anne of Green Gables for her spunk in breaking that slate over Gilbert Blythe's head.

What was your favorite thing about school?

It's sort of weird and nerdy to say this, but I loved almost everything about school, and during summer vacations, I'd even cross off the days until school started again. Best of all, I loved any writing assignments and being in plays. In fifth grade, I played the role of stuck-up cousin Annabelle in our classroom play of *Caddie Woodlawn*, and that was wonderful.

What was your least favorite thing about school?
Definitely PE! I was always terrible at PE. I just couldn't do any of the sports, and one time the fourth-grade teacher made the whole class stop and look over at how terribly I was doing this one exercise. I still hate her for that.

What were your hobbies as a kid? What are your hobbies now?
Well, writing, definitely, and reading and taking long walks. Hey, those are my same hobbies now. The only new hobby I've added is obsessively checking e-mail.

What was your first job, and what was your "worst" job?
My first job was working in the junior clothes department at Sears. Back then, three girls worked in one department: one to work the cash register, one to oversee the dressing room, and one to tidy up the clothes racks. I loved tidying up the clothes racks, buttoning up the dresses that needed buttoning. I loved buttoning one dress so much that I bought it, and then found that once I had it at home I had no desire to button it at all anymore. My worst job was being a waitress. I would have done all right if I could have handled just one table at a time, from drinks to salad to main course and

then dessert, but my brain could not handle juggling all those different tables at once.

How did you celebrate publishing your first book?

I don't remember celebrating it. Now that I look back, I wish I had. It's a very special moment.

Where do you write your books?

I write all my books in longhand, lying on the couch, using the same clipboard-without-a-clip that I've had for thirty years, always using a white narrow-ruled pad with no margins, and always using a Pilot Razor Point fine-tipped black marker pen.

What sparked your imagination for *How Oliver Olson Changed the World*?

Whenever I visit schools as an author, I love to walk up and down the hallways and look at whatever student work is posted there. In one school, I saw that the kids had completed an assignment where they had to write their ideas for how they would change the world. Bingo! I was all set and ready to go! Then I had to decide who my main character would be, and I decided that I should pick a kid who would be initially exceedingly unlikely to change the world. Many of the kids I know today are very overprotected by their parents, so I decided to make Oliver a kid with hovering "helicopter parents" who do everything for him so that he can never do anything for himself. A dear friend who is that kind of parent knew I was working on the book, and she told me, "If you need any more information about overprotective parents, just come over to our house!"

Of the books you've written, which is your favorite?

I don't have a favorite. My books feel like my children; each one has such a huge piece of my heart in it. So I wouldn't want to hurt their feelings by loving one of them more than its brothers and sisters.

What challenges do you face in the writing process, and how do you overcome them?

By far the biggest challenge is learning how to accept, and even to welcome, criticism. I hate criticism and always want everybody to love my books from the very first draft. But the only way to grow as a writer, and to produce the best possible book, is to listen to what critical readers tell you, and then rewrite, rewrite, rewrite.

Which of your characters is most like you?

Each one is like me in some way, or maybe I become more like that character as I write about him or her. I think overall the two who are most like me are Dinah in the Dinah books and Lizzie in *Lizzie at Last*. Lizzie is so much like me that I even dedicated the book to myself: "For the girl I used to be."

What makes you laugh out loud?

I always laugh out loud if somebody is trying to do something in an oh-so-serious way and then something goes hideously and publicly awry. That kind of thing makes me howl.

What do you do on a rainy day?
Write and read, of course!

What's your idea of fun?
Writing and reading!

What's your favorite song?
Gosh, I have so many. I guess I'll go with "Here Comes the Sun" by The Beatles.

Who is your favorite fictional character?
Betsy Ray in the Betsy-Tacy books by Maud Hard Lovelace

What was your favorite book when you were a kid? Do you have a favorite book now?
It was and still is *Betsy and Tacy Go Downtown* by Maud Hart Lovelace, which I consider to be the finest novel in the English language.

What's your favorite TV show or movie?
I don't watch much TV. My favorite movie, in recent years, is *Julie & Julia*; I loved watching both women develop as writers.

If you were stranded on a desert island, who would you want for company?
I'd be happy with pretty much anybody. In elementary school, the teachers would keep moving my desk so I'd

stop talking to the person next to me, but then they found out that I would be happy talking to anyone.

If you could travel anywhere in the world, where would you go and what would you do?
I'd like to live in Paris, in a garret, and write, and be very poor, and make money by selling flowers on the street corner.

If you could travel in time, where would you go and what would you do?
I'd go back to Amherst, Massachusetts, in the 1850s, and walk by Emily Dickinson's house, and see if she would lower a little basket out the window to me with a fresh-baked muffin and a freshly written poem in it.

What's the best advice you have ever received about writing?
Brenda Ueland says, in *If You Want to Write*, that writing is supposed to be fun, and that if we allow ourselves to let it be fun, stories and poems will just keep pouring out of us. I think she's right.

Do you ever get writer's block? What do you do to get back on track?
I don't, really. My secret is to write for a short, fixed time—usually an hour—every single day. That way I never get burned out from writing, and I never get far enough away from my story that I lose my momentum.

What do you want readers to remember about your books?

I always try to have my main character learn a small but important truth about how to make his or her life better. Oliver learns that even if he can't change the whole world, he can change some little part of it. But I know when I think back to favorite books I read a long time ago, it tends to be some little, trivial-but-fun detail that sticks in my head.

What would you do if you ever stopped writing?

Oh, I hope I never do! But I do love reading almost as much, so I guess I'd just read, read, read. Or teach writing, which I do already and love doing.

What do you like best about yourself?

I am very good at being cheerful. I have all kinds of strategies and techniques and lists and mantras that I use to cheer myself up when I have hard things to deal with in my life. I think I have a gift for making myself reasonably happy.

Do you have any strange or funny habits? Did you when you were a kid?

I chew my pen or pencil as I write—I always have. Once, a few years ago, I chewed my pen so hard while I was writing that I broke my tooth and had to spend five hundred dollars at the dentist to get it fixed.

What do you consider to be your greatest accomplishment?
I'm proud that I've written over forty books while always working full-time at another demanding profession (being a university professor of philosophy).

What do you wish you could do better?
I wish I could cook. The meals at my house are horrible. I pretty much live on English muffins with butter and orange marmalade.

What would your readers be most surprised to learn about you?
My favorite food is candy, particularly seasonal candy: candy corn at Halloween, those little Conversation Hearts for Valentine's Day, Cadbury Creme Eggs at Easter.

Riley O'Rourke falls in love with the sax, but his mom
says they can't afford to rent the instrument. But as he
prepares for the dreaded fourth-grade biography tea, Riley
realizes that there may be a solution to his problem after
all. Teddy Roosevelt never gave up and neither will he!

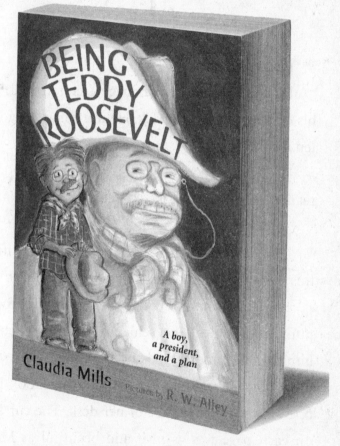

Keep reading for an excerpt from

BEING TEDDY ROOSEVELT

by Claudia Mills

1

Riley gave up.

He couldn't find his language arts notebook in his desk or in his backpack. He must have forgotten it somewhere.

"Does everybody have his or her notebook ready?" Mrs. Harrow asked. "Riley?"

"I think I left it at home."

Mrs. Harrow sighed. "This is the third time this week that you're missing a notebook, Riley."

Riley was impressed that she knew the exact number of times. She remembered more about him than he remembered about himself.

Sophie sat on Riley's right. Her notebook lay open in the exact middle of her desk. The cursive on each page was as neat and beautiful as Mrs. Harrow's on the chalkboard.

Erika sat on Riley's left. She had her notebook out, but she hadn't opened it. Erika did only what she felt like doing. Apparently, she didn't feel like opening her notebook right now.

Riley's best friend, Grant, sat directly in front of Riley. His notebook was almost as perfect as Sophie's. Grant's parents bought him a video game for every A he got on his report card. Riley didn't think he could get A's even if his mother bought him ten video games for each one. He had a hard enough time getting B's and C's.

Mrs. Harrow handed Riley a piece of paper. "You can write your assignment on this."

Of course, now Riley would have to make sure he didn't lose the piece of paper.

"Don't lose it, dear," Mrs. Harrow said.

"All right, class," she went on. "We are going to be starting our fall unit on biographies. Does anyone know what a biography is?"

Sophie did. "It's a book about someone's life. A true book. About a famous person's life."

Sophie would probably have a biography written

about her someday—if a person could be famous for having a neat notebook and 100 percent on every spelling test. *Sophie Sartin: The Girl Who Never Made a Mistake*. That would be the title.

Riley meant to listen to what Mrs. Harrow was saying next, but he couldn't stop thinking up titles for other biographies.

Erika Lee: The Girl Who Did What She Wanted. He noticed that Erika still hadn't opened her notebook. Mrs. Harrow hadn't said anything to her about it, either.

Grant Littleton: The Boy Who Owned Every Single Video Game System Ever Invented. Plus Every Single Game. Not a very short or snappy title, but a lot of kids would want to read that one.

What would the title of his biography be? *Riley O'Rourke: The Boy Who Couldn't Find His Notebook*. That didn't sound like a book kids would be lining up to read. *Riley O'Rourke: The Boy Who Would Forget His Head If It Weren't Fastened On*.

That's what grownups were always saying to him: "Riley, you'd forget your head if it weren't fastened on." The book would have cool illustrations, at least. There could be a picture of a seal balancing Riley's head on its nose like a beach ball. Or someone dunking his head into the hoop at a basketball game.

Riley grinned.

"Remember, class," Mrs. Harrow said, "the biography you read has to be at least one hundred pages long. Your five-page report on the biography is due three weeks from today, on Wednesday, October fourth. And then on that Friday we'll have our fourth-grade biography tea."

"What's a biography tea?" Sophie asked.

Mrs. Harrow gave the class a big smile. It was clear that she thought a biography tea was something extremely wonderful. Right away, Riley got a sinking feeling in the pit of his stomach.

"On the day of our biography tea," Mrs. Harrow said, "you will arrive at school dressed up as the subject of your biography. All day long you will act like that person. Then in the afternoon we will have a fancy tea party, and you famous people from world history will sit at special decorated tables and have tea together!"

To say that Riley would rather die than go to a biography tea would be an exaggeration. But not a big exaggeration.

Sophie gave a little squeal of delight. "I love tea parties!"

Erika gave a little snort of disgust. Riley gathered that Erika did not love tea parties.

Grant raised his hand. "We can be whoever we want, right?"

Mrs. Harrow shook her head. "Oh, no, dear. I let the children pick one year, and I got only football players and rock stars. I've prepared two hats filled with names, one for boys and one for girls. You will draw from the hats to find out the subject of your biography."

For the first time, Riley noticed two hats perched on Mrs. Harrow's desk. The black stovepipe Abe Lincoln hat must be for the boys. The flowered straw hat must be for the girls.

The first girl to choose got Pocahontas, an Indian princess.

The first boy to choose got Napoleon, the French emperor.

Sophie got Helen Keller, the blind and deaf woman. She didn't squeal with delight this time.

Erika got Florence Nightingale. "Who's Florence Nightingale?"

"She was a famous nurse," Mrs. Harrow said.

"I don't want to be a nurse."

"Well . . ." Riley knew Mrs. Harrow would give in. That was the only way of dealing with Erika. "I suppose you could be Queen Elizabeth the First."

Riley hoped he'd get some famous musician, like Beethoven or Duke Ellington, or even better, a sax player like Charlie Parker.

He got President Teddy Roosevelt. That wasn't too bad. Riley had seen a picture of Teddy Roosevelt once, wearing a uniform and sitting on a horse. But reading a hundred-page book about Teddy Roosevelt and writing a five-page paper about Teddy Roosevelt and trying to drink tea while wearing a mustache would be terrible.

Grant got Mahatma Gandhi.

"Gandhi!" Grant shouted. "The bald guy who sits cross-legged on the ground in his underwear?"

"Gandhi, the great man who liberated India from the British," Mrs. Harrow corrected.

"Who liberated India from the British while sitting cross-legged on the ground in his underwear," Grant moaned.

Riley knew Grant wanted to refuse to be Gandhi. But only Erika ever refused to do things in school. Maybe Grant's parents would buy him an extra game for having to be Gandhi.

When everyone had drawn a name, Mrs. Harrow gave the class another big smile. "I can't wait for this year's biography tea!"

Riley could wait. A tea party with Pocahontas, Napoleon, Helen Keller, Queen Elizabeth I, Mahatma Gandhi, and Teddy Roosevelt?

No way!